THE JAGS

A New Striker

TOM WATT

Text, design and layout © 2009 Rising Stars Uk Ltd.
The right of Tom Watt to be identified as the author of this work has been asserted by him in accordance with the Copyright, Design and Patents Act, 1988.

Published 2009

Publisher: Gill Budgell
Editor: Jane Wood
Text design and typesetting: Clive Sutherland
Illustrator: Michael Emmerson for Advocate Art
Cover design: Burville-Riley Partnership
Cover photograph: Ron Coello at www.coellophotography.co.uk
With special thanks to; Robert Dye, Harry Garner, Tyrone Smith, Lewis McKenzie, Kobina Crankson and Alex Whyte

British Library Cataloguing in Publication Data.
A CIP record for this book is available from the British Library.

ISBN: 978-1-84680-477-9

Printed in the UK by CPI Bookmarque, Croydon, CR0 4TD

Mixed Sources
Product group from well-managed forests and other controlled sources
www.fsc.org Cert no. TT-COC-002227
© 1996 Forest Stewardship Council
FSC

2

Contents

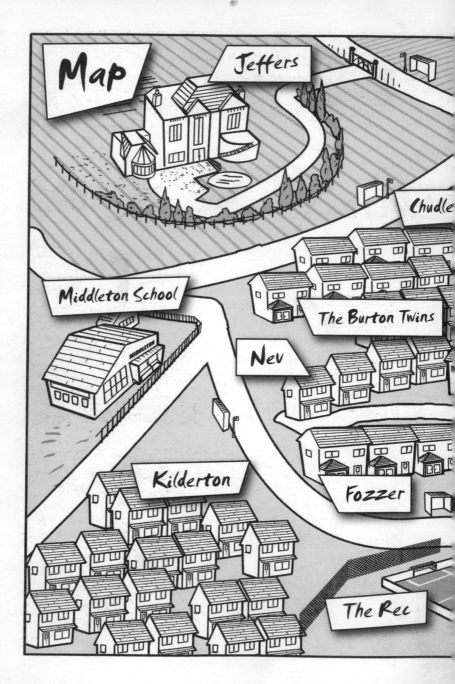

Upton Prep School

The Vale

Park

Keeps

Dev

Valley Road Stadium

Parkside School

Meet the Jags

Andy

Name: Andrew Burton

Fact: He's the Jags' captain.

Loves: Spurs

FYI: The Jags may be his mates, but they'd better not forget he's the Skipper.

Burts

Name: Terry Burton

Fact: He's Andy's twin brother.

Loves: Football, football, and more football. He's football crazy!

FYI: He's a big Arsenal fan.

Dev

Name: Ryan Devlin

Fact: He's very forgetful.

Loves: Daydreaming!

FYI: He's always covered in mud and bruises.

Fozzer

Name: Hamed Foster

Fact: He can run like crazy, but he shoots like crazy too – sometimes at the wrong goal!

Loves: Telling bad jokes.

FYI: His best friend is Nev.

Keeps

Name: Jim Ward

Fact: He's the Jags' Number One goalie – whether he likes it or not!

Loves: Trying to score from his end of the pitch.

FYI: He's the tallest member of the Jags.

Jeffers

Name: Jeffrey Gilfoyle Chapman

Fact: He's the only one of the Jags who doesn't live on the Chudley Park estate.

Loves: Being in the Jags.

FYI: He's the Jags' top goal-scorer.

Nev

Name: Denton Neville

Fact: Nev is the Jags' most talented player.

Loves: Fozzer's bad jokes.

FYI: He keeps his feet on the ground and always looks out for his football crazy mates.

Mrs Burton

Name: Pam Burton

Fact: The Burton twins' mum, and a team 'mum' for all the Jags.

Loves: Sorting out her boys.

FYI: Doesn't actually like football!

Mr Ward

Name: Jack Ward

Fact: He's Jim's dad and the Jags' coach!

Loves: Going on and on, doing his team talks.

FYI: He's taking his coaching exams.

First Timer

Jeffers is the only member of the Jags who doesn't live on the estate. He's my best mate now, but I remember when we first met. It was at a holiday soccer school at Valley Road. My brother, Burts, was sick, so I needed a partner for the warm-ups. And there was this lad, called Jeffrey, wearing a Spurs top like me.

Andy   All right, Jeffrey? Do you need a
           partner for the warm-ups?

Jeffers Yes, I think so. How does it work?

Andy   Haven't you been to a soccer
           school before?

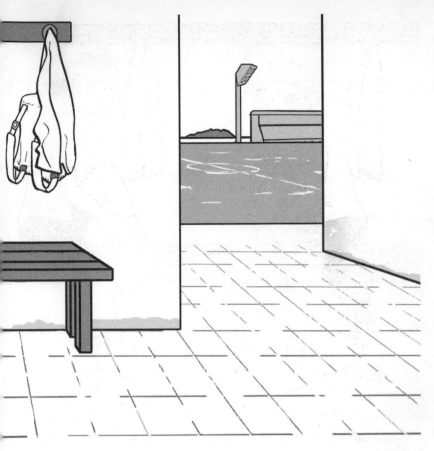

Jeffers No. I just saw it in the local paper and thought I'd give it a try.

Andy What do you usually do in the holidays, then?

Jeffers Oh, we go to our villa in Spain.

Andy   That sounds nice. But if you like football, this is the place to be. Come on. Are you ready?

Jeffers   Yes, thank you. I'll just follow what you do, shall I?

Andy   Well, we usually start with a
             warm-up. That's unless we get
             Mr Ward. Then we have to sit
             round and he does a lot of
             talking before we even start!

Jeffers I don't think I know Mr Ward.

Andy   Lucky you. He loves talking tactics, even when we just want to play a game. He's all right, really. And he coaches the Jaguars.

Jeffers   The Jaguars?

Andy   Shhh. They're starting. I'll have to tell you later.

A Great Idea!

So Andy told me all about his football team, the Chudley Park Jaguars. I must say I was jealous. We don't have a team at my school. They're more into touch rugby at Upton Prep.

Andy   Who's your favourite player, then?

Jeffers Gerald, I suppose.

Andy Gerald? Is he Spurs' new signing?

Jeffers No, no. He's the only other boy at my school who likes football as much as I do.

Andy   But you *are* a Spurs fan, aren't you?

Jeffers   Um, no. Not really. This is just the shirt my mother gave me to wear. I don't really have a team I support.

I could see I had a bit of work to do here. But maybe I could get this lad to be a Spurs fan, too. There aren't many of us round here.

Andy   What about Aaron Lennon?
He's got lots of tricks like you.

Jeffers   Oh, yes. I know him all right.
I've seen him do this on TV.

Andy   That's good. That's what he does
when he scores.

Jeffers   I like trying things that I've seen players do on TV.

Andy   Like what?

Jeffers   Um, well. Stay there, and then I'll run at you with the ball.

Andy   I couldn't tell which way you were going to go.

Jeffers   That's the idea.

Andy   And who did you see doing that?

Jeffers   Lionel Messi. He did it in La Liga last weekend.

A Box of Tricks

> Later on we had five-a-side games. And Jeffrey was great. He scored a hat-trick. Nobody got near him.

Andy   That was fun.

Jeffers   Fun? That was great!

Andy   For the first goal, that step-over was really good.

Jeffers I copied it from Christiano Ronaldo.

Andy   What about the free kick?

Jeffers I saw Michael Ballack do that at the Euros.

Andy And the volley? Don't tell me. Michael Owen?

Jeffers Well, no, not really. I just made that up.

Andy Well, you were man of the match, anyway.

Jeffers Oh, I don't know. It's not just goals, is it? You put in some great tackles, Andrew.

Andy   You can call me Andy. That's
               what the other Jags call me.
               What's your nickname?

Jeffers   I don't really have a nickname.

Andy   But every player has a
               nickname.

Jeffers   Do they?

Andy   Oh, yeah. Now, let me think.
Jeffrey. Jeff. What about
"Jeffers"? That sounds quite
posh. But it does sound like a
footballer's nickname.

Jeffers   "Jeffers"? Yes. I think I could get
used to that.

Andy   Now all you need are some team-mates to call you that. Are you here again tomorrow, Jeffers?

Jeffers   I hope so. I'll have to ask my dad.

Andy   Well, I'll talk to you then. I think I might have a great idea ...

Jeffers   All right. See you tomorrow, Andrew. I mean Andy!

Sign Him Up!

As soon as I got home, I got the lads together at the Rec. I told them I had found the Jags a star striker. Now all I had to do was get Jeffers to join us!

Andy   It's ten past ten and he's still not here. Maybe his dad wouldn't let him come to the soccer school again.

Jeffers   Hello, Andy.

Andy   Hello, Jeffers. I thought you weren't coming.

Jeffers   I had to finish some homework before breakfast.

Andy   Homework? Before breakfast?

Jeffers It's a project I had to finish.

Andy Don't you ever get any time off?

Jeffers Oh, yes. I should have finished it before the holidays. My dad said I couldn't come to the soccer school again until I finished it. So I did.

Andy So you might have a bit of time to play football?

Jeffers What, today? I should hope so. That's why I'm here.

Andy   No. I don't just mean today.

Jeffers   Why? Is there soccer school again tomorrow? I thought it was just for two days.

Andy   I don't mean soccer school. I mean playing for a football team.

Jeffers   There aren't enough boys at my school who want to play for a football team. Just me and Gerald.

Andy   I know a team, though. The Jags. Remember?

Jeffers   I know. You're lucky. It must be great to have a game every week.

Andy   Sometimes we play more than one a week. And then there's the training as well.

Jeffers   That must be more fun than just watching football on TV and then playing on my own in the garden.

Andy   Well, you'll never know unless you try it.

Jeffers   What do you mean?

Andy   I mean what about joining the Jags? We need a goal-scorer. I talked to the others last night and we think you might be our man.

Jeffers   What? *Me*, play for the Chudley Park Jaguars?

Andy   Yeah. What do you think?

Jeffers   Jeffers a Jag? Whoopee!

Andy   Shall I take that as a "yes", Jeffers?

The Line-up

> It took Jeffers a while to take it in. Later on, I told him a bit more about the team.

Jeffers   Did you mean it about me playing for the Jags?

Andy   Well, you'd have to come for a trial. But from what I've seen, that won't be a problem.

Jeffers   Great!

Andy   But would you be able to come
            over to Chudley Park to play?

Jeffers   Try stopping me!

Andy   Great. Well, let me tell you a bit
            more about the team. Keeps is
            our goalie and his dad, Jack
            Ward, is our coach. He talks
            about tactics *all* the time.

Keeps

Jack

Andy   Then there's my brother, Burts. And Fozzer and Nev. They're good players, but when we're not playing, they're always joking around.

Jeffers   I'll watch out for them, then!

Andy   And then there's Dev and Mrs Burton.

Jeffers   Is Mrs Burton his mum?

Andy   No. She's *my* mum and Terry's mum. Our mum. Her name's Pam.

Jeffers   Why do you call her Mrs Burton?

Andy   Well, that's her football name, when she's helping Mr Ward with the Jags. At home, we just call her mum. What do you think?

Jeffers   I think I'll call her Mrs Burton.

Andy   No, I mean what do you think about joining the Jags?

Jeffers   Mmm. Just one question, really, Andy. When can I start?

JAGUARS 4 MARSDEN 2

Jeffers plays for us every week now. I still remember his first game. We were playing a good team from Marsden Road. They had beaten us the last two times we played them. But this time we had Jeffers!

Jeffers   Great pass, Andy!

Andy   Great shot, Jeffers. That makes it
3–1 to the Jags. And you've
scored a hat-trick!

Jeffers   How long have we still got left?

Andy   Why? How many more goals do
            you want to score?

Jeffers It's not that, Andy. I just want to
             keep on playing. This is great!

It ended up 4–2 to the Jags. Nev scored the other goal. It was a great game and a great result. The lads were happy that I'd found a new striker. And our new striker was happy that he'd found us!

Star Strikers

Strikers are forwards. Strikers are the stars of modern football. Their job is to score the goals. Every striker is different. Some are tall. Some are strong. Some are left-footed. Some are right-footed. Some are good with their heads. Some are fast. Some are clever.

The best striker is one who has a bit of everything, of course!

 There are lots of ways to score a goal.

 A striker can score with his feet.

 If a cross comes over, he can score with a header.

 If the ball is in the air, the striker can shoot before it hits the ground. That's called a volley.

 Sometimes a striker scores with a free kick. Or maybe he takes all his team's penalties.

 Who do you think is the best striker in the Premier League? Waney

Rooney of corse!!

The Goal!!! Quiz

Questions

1 Is a striker a forward or a defender?
2 What is a striker's job?
3 Where does the ball have to go for a striker to score?
4 Who does the striker try to get the ball past?
5 What do we call it when a striker scores three goals in a game?

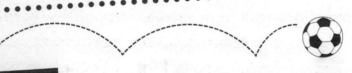

Answers

1 A forward.
2 Scoring goals.
3 Between the posts and under the bar – in the goal!
4 The goalkeeper.
5 A hat-trick.

About the Author

Tom Watt, who writes the Jags books, used to play right-back for his team. That means he was trying to stop goals, not score them. He is too old to play for a team now. That's what his son tells him. So he plays in the back garden instead.

Tom's son is a good goalie, so Tom sometimes takes shots. They go in the hedge. Or over the wall. Or through the window. About 1 in 20 of Tom's shots goes in the goal. That's why he used to be a right-back and not a striker.

THE JAGS

RISING ★ STARS